PEEL,
the
Extraordinary
Elephant

by
Susan Joyce

Illustrations by
D.C. DuBosque

Peel Productions
P.O. Box 11500
Portland, Oregon 97211

Library of Congress Catalog Number 86-61990
ISBN 0-939217-00-7 (Library hard cover)
ISBN 0-939217-01-5 (Sewn paperback)

First American Edition 1988
10 9 8 7 6 5 4 3 2 1

Printed in
Singapore

Library of Congress Cataloging-in-Publication Data

Joyce, Susan, 1945-
    Peel, the extraordinary elephant.

    Summary: A young elephant, straying from his herd,
picks up his trunk and sets out in search of adventure.
    [1. Elephants--Fiction. 2. Animals--Fiction. 3. Stories
in rhyme] I. DuBosque, D. C. , Ill. II. Title.

PZ8. 3. J83Pe   1988   [E]   86-61990
ISBN 0-939217-00-7 (lib. bdg.)
ISBN 0-939217-01-5 (pbk.)

For Jane, Michael, Jody, Van
and all the "extraordinary" creatures
who have cared enough to teach me.

Special thanks to Dr. Jane Lannak, whose thoughtful editing has influenced both writing and illustrations.

CHAPTER ONE

AN ELEPHANT WON'T FORGET

"Ho-hummm," the elephant rolled to and fro,
stretching his trunk, as far as it would go,

> *"An elephant won't…"*

he stared at the sky,
trying hard to remember the old lullaby.

> *"An elephant won't forget you…*
> *when you're happy."*

He looked all around, in hopes of a cheer.
But he'd strayed from his herd and no one was near.

He stamped his foot, hard, shaking the ground.
"It's lonely," he muttered, "with no one around.."

"Why can't I remember the rest of the rhyme?"
Patting his head, he tried one more time.

"An elephant won't forget you when you're happy.
An elephant won't forget you when you're sad."

A dandelion puffball floated close by.
When it tickled his toes he chuckled, "Oh my!"

Carefully sniffing, he bounced it about,
grinned when it tickled his sensitive snout.

With a swirl and a twirl it danced on the ledge.
When he laughed out loud, it fell off the edge.

"Oh no," he moaned, "what a long way to fall."

"Ohhhhhhh, no-no-nooo…" said the valley, repeating his call.

He waited a moment, then called out, "H-e-l-l-o?"

The mountain side echoed, "H-e-l-lo-lo-lo-lo…"

As the wind whispered gently, the sun lost its glow.
And the elephant wondered, "What's down there below?
Could it be a secret place, where no one's ever been?"
When he thought of secrets, the rhyme came back to him.

"An elephant won't forget you when you're happy.
An elephant won't forget you when you're sad.
'Cause an elephant knows the secret…
is remembering it all.
Learning from the good times and the bad."

"Hooray!" He jumped up, almost touching a cloud.
"I remember it all," he shouted out loud.

Then he picked up his trunk and he trotted along
down the steep mountain side, proudly singing his song.

CHAPTER TWO

PEEL MEETS CAMILLE

"Sluuuuuuurrrrrpppp."

A sound from nearby jarred him awake.
A strange slurping sound, from down by the lake.

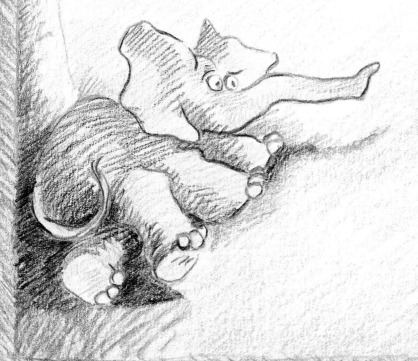

"Sluuuuuuurrrrpppp. Sluuuuuuurrrrpppp."

To his great surprise, a creature stood there
a bump on its back and with brown stubby hair.

He stared at the bump and thought for a minute,
"something that big must have something in it."

Waltzing toward him, she noticed his stare.
"It's a hump," she smiled, "I store my food there.

My name is Camille," her eyelashes fluttered.

"A-a-a-a-an-nd I'm an elephant," he stammered and stuttered.

"Darling, that's plain to see.
 But, what is your name?"

"I am an elephant. That is my name."

"I am a camel, but Camille is my name.
 Perhaps you've forgotten, let me explain…
 A camel's a breed, with a hump on its back.
 Nothing unique, just one of the pack.
 A who, not a what, is important to be.
 A name of your own makes you special, you see."

"A name of my own? That sounds very elegant.
I've always just thought of myself as an elephant."

"Nonsense," she sputtered, "that's hardly the same.
Give me a moment, I'll find you a name.
There was one, I recall, from a long time before…
Oh dear, I forgot. But, I know hundreds more.
There's Sylvester, Rasputin, Aladdin, Kilgore?"

"Oh never," he moaned. "Do you know any more?"

"Well, there's Robert, Reynaldo, Ringo and Jed,
Zachery, Thackeray, Milton and Ted."

"Milton?" he bellowed, expanding his chest.
She continued her search for the name that fit best.

"…It's hard to recall all the places I've been,
the faces, the names, just where they fit in."

Not remember? How silly, the elephant thought.
There is nothing I've done that I've ever forgot.

"It starts with a P," she sniffed all around.
"It's four letters long," her paw scratched the ground.
"It ends with an L and sounds like a bell."
She smiled, then she said, "I remember it well.

It suits you exactly. Just perfect, I feel."
Then matter of factly, she christened him…"Peel!"

An el - e - phant won't for - get you when you're sad.

CHAPTER THREE

PEEL AND THE ANT

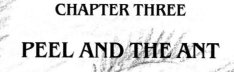

Twitching and itching, Peel started to shake.
A screeching and screaming jarred him awake.

His big eyes crossed as she stomped up his trunk.
"You're wrecking our city! You BIG CLUMSY CLUNK!"

"I couldn't," Peel mumbled, wiping sleep from his eyes.
"There isn't a city, for miles, besides…"

"Elephants are dumbos," she glared, "You just play.
Ants work. We build cities and harvest each day.
Then YOU come along and plop yourself down
and toss your fat trunk on top of our town."

"But, I didn't know," Peel stared at his toes,
"that a city was sitting right under my nose."

His eyes filled with tears, both ears drooping down,
"I'm sorry," he sobbed, "for wrecking your town."

"Don't cry," the ant pleaded. "You'll just start a flood.
Our queen ant is resting. She doesn't like mud."

Peel sniffled and snurfled, the ant wiped his eyes dry.
"Forgive me," she whispered, "for making you cry."

Then she twirled on his trunk and toe-danced awhile,
with a bow, she proclaimed, "I want you to smile!"

Peel grinned, "You're terrific! I wish I could dance.
But when you're my size, there's really no chance.
You're delicate, nimble, lovely and small.
I guess I am a clumsy clunk…

Too **B I G,** too *ROUND*, too TALL."

"I'll teach you," she said. "It's easy, you'll see.
I'm sure you can learn to dance just like me.

Now, watch my legs closely, I'll show you my tricks.
One, two, three and four, and of course…five and six."

Peel groaned, "I'm confused! If I had two legs more,
perhaps I could dance, but I only have four."

"We do have a problem." She crossed her legs and thought…
and thought… and thought…
and wondered if an elephant could ever be taught.

Then she rubbed her legs in glee, "I've got it, I know.
I'll teach you to tiptoe. Are you ready, let's go."

So Peel learned to tiptoe, lightly on his toes,
careful where he put his feet and where he tossed his nose.

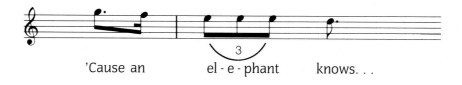

'Cause an   el - e - phant   knows. . .

CHAPTER FOUR

PEEL LEARNS TO SWIM

Peel knelt beside the river and watched the ripples swim.
He saw a great big elephant looking back at him.

"You look like me," he whispered as the water swirled.
Peel curled his trunk, to his surprise, the other also curled.

Then deep down in the water, he glimpsed a golden light.
He swung his trunk to catch it, but it flashed out of sight.

Peel dunked his head and looked around, his big eyes open wide.
"Ah-ha," he said, "I see you. Now don't you try to hide!"

A golden fish circled round, filled her gills and giggled.
"Elephants stay close to shore," she flipped her fins, then wiggled.

"My name is Peel," he stared at her and sadly shook his head.
"If I had fins, then I could swim, but I have feet instead."

"But you can learn, just use your feet. To swim I move my tail.
 Courage is what you really need. With courage you can't fail."

Peel watched the golden fish glide past, glistening in the sun.
She turned and waved her flowing tail, "Swimming is great fun."

He plunged into the river. Waves banged and bashed the shore.
Peel kicked his feet and paddled fast, then trumpeted a roar.

"Hooray! Hooray! You learned to swim," the fish was cheering loudly.
"You taught me how," he smiled at her, "Thank you," he said proudly.

... the sec - ret   is   re -   mem - ber - ing   it   all.

CHAPTER FIVE

THE EXTRAORDINARY OWL

By the glow of a moon, night creatures came creeping.
To hunt for their food while the jungle lay sleeping.

Peel found a soft spot and he lay down to sleep.
"Ninety-nine, eighty-seven," he counted his sheep.

Then a voice loud and clear made him shake with fright.
"WHOOO, WHOO ARE YOUOOOO?" asked the voice in the night.

Peel opened his eyes and he looked everywhere.
To the left, to the right, but no one was there.

The voice in the night called to him again,
in a deep husky howl, "WHOOO, WHOOO," it began.

Peel looked up in the trees. Two eyes brightly glared.
He took a deep breath. The wide-eyed owl stared.

"I am an elephant. But, Peel is my name.
Listen a moment? I can explain…
An elephant's a breed, with a trunk and broad back.
Nothing unique, just one of a pack.
A who, not a what, is important to be.
A name of your own makes you special, you see?"

"Whooooo," said the owl, her wing tips flaring,
"is what you become by learning and sharing.
You're more than an elephant whose name is Peel.
You're all that you know and all that you feel.
Take elephants or owls, we all are unique.
In the way that we move, in the way that we speak.
A who and a what are important to be.
But learning is what makes you extraordinary, you see."

Before Peel could speak, the owl flew away.
He ran after her, there was so much to say.

"Extraordinary," shouted Peel, "what a wonderful word!"
He called up to her, "Is it true what I heard?"

Peel waved from the hill at the owl in the moon.
He had so many questions. She had left him too soon.

Learn - ing   from the   good times   and   the   bad.

CHAPTER SIX

PEEL AND CAMILLE

Peel travelled along over dry barren sands,
crossing jungles and valleys and green grassy lands.

Sometimes he felt lonely, sometimes he felt sad.
But when Peel sang his song, he always felt glad.

"An elephant won't forget you…"

One hot summer day, Peel lay down to rest,
carefully tossing his trunk cross his chest.
He daydreamed, then drifted into a deep sleep
before he could even begin to count sheep.

"Sluuuuuuurrrrpppp."

A sound from nearby jarred him awake.
A strange slurping sound, from down by the lake.

"Sluuuuuuurrrrpppp. Sluuuuuuurrrrpppp."

To his great surprise, a camel stood there,
a hump on her back and with brown stubby hair.

He stared at the hump and thought for a minute.
"I know that hump, she keeps her food in it."

Shuffling toward her, he noticed her stare.
"Camille," he called out, "Is that you standing there?"

"I am Camille," her eyelashes fluttered.
"Have we met before?" she stammered and stuttered.

"Oh yes," Peel replied. "We met years ago.
You gave me my name…"

She blinked, "Is that so?"

"…It's hard to recall all the places I've been,
the faces, the names, just where they fit in.
There was one I recall, from a long time before…
Oh dear, I forgot. But I know hundreds more.
There's Sylvester, Rasputin, Aladdin, Kilgore?"

Peel grinned at her, "Do you know any more?"

"Well, there's Robert, Reynaldo, Ringo and Jed,
Zachery, Thackeray, Milton and Ted."

"I'll give you some clues," Peel thumped his thick chest.
"It starts with a P and fits me the best."

"It starts with a P?" Camille sniffed the ground.

"It's four letters long," Peel swung his trunk round.

Camille smiled at him, "It ends with an L."

Peel nodded his head, "…and it sounds like a bell."

"It suits you exactly. Just perfect, I feel."
Then matter of factly she said to him, "Peel,
how lovely to see you. How big you have grown.
Tell me, what have you done, these years on your own?"

"I've learned many things." Peel smiled and exclaimed.
"I know how to swim," he proudly proclaimed.

"Delightful," said Camille. "Oh please tell me more."

Peel stood on his toes, "I tiptoe on all four…"

Camille smiled at him, softly chewing her cud.
"…and, I learned that a queen ant doesn't like mud.
I've learned we're unique. Each in our own way.
By learning and sharing, we grow every day.
I'll always remember the day we first met.
You made me feel special. I'll never forget."

"How nice you remembered," her eyes filled with tears.

"An elephant won't forget you, not in a million years."

They trotted off together, Peel teaching her his song.

"An elephant won't forget you…"

Camille sang along.

Printed in Singapore through Palace Press